GLEN NELSON

Sock Drawer Wands

PRIVATE DRAGON
Publishing

First published by Private Dragon Publishing 2021

Copyright © 2021 by Glen Nelson

This novel is entirely a work of fiction. The names, characters and incidents portrayed in it are the work of the author's imagination. Any resemblance to actual persons, living or dead, events or localities is entirely coincidental.

First edition

ISBN: 978-1-951405-21-2

Editing by Jake Lueckler
Cover art by Samantha Knight

This book was professionally typeset on Reedsy.
Find out more at reedsy.com

Contents

Chapter 1

Chester Thomas stood in the hallway and listened to his parents talk with an FBI agent in the living room. As he listened, he recalled the event they were discussing.

He was only four years old when it happened. He would often sneak into his parents' room and look inside one of his father's sock drawers. It was filled with interesting things and smelled of cedarwood and cologne. There was an old tin that used to contain hair pomade in which his dad now put coins. There were some sticks that his dad whittled when he was a boy. A lint brush that Chester would brush his hair with and make it stand on-end with static. His favorite item was a wooden toy that his father had as a boy.

Chester could handle the things in the drawer, but he could never take them out of the room. On this day, however, he took the toy to his room to play with. It was a little wooden bombing scope with crosshairs and a wheel to turn to release little wooden bombs. He laid some targets on the floor and looked through the bomb site and was ready to release the first bomb when he heard his father's voice in the hall.

Chester hadn't heard the car pull into the driveway or the front door open when his dad came in, nor did he remember dropping the toy or throwing it behind anything, but when his dad poked his head into Chester's room to say "hi" the toy was gone. He felt some relief that he was not caught with it but felt dread in his father finding it missing from his drawer.

"You look worried," his dad said, walking into his room.

Chester looked all around his room and said, "I forgot."

"What did you forget?" his dad asked.

"I don't know," he answered. "I forgot."

His dad gripped his arms, just below the shoulders as he had done many times, and lifted him gently to the ceiling.

"If you don't think about it, you'll remember," he soothed, placing Chester on his back.

He carried Chester into the kitchen where he kissed his wife then walked to his bedroom. Chester knew what his dad was about to do. He was going to open his drawer and place coins in the old tin. Chester was about to confess what he had done with the toy when his dad opened the drawer. Chester drew a quick breath when he saw the bomber toy in its place.

"Did you remember?" his dad asked.

"Yeah," he replied with relief.

His dad put him on the ground, opened the pomade can, and deposited the coins. Chester left the room happy yet confused. His mind was brought back to the present by his mother calling him into the front room. He entered the living room and walked toward his mother.

The agent stood and stepped between Chester and his mother.

He put out his hand toward Chester and introduced himself, "I'm special agent Dobson."

Chester shook the agent's hand, nodded politely, then sat next to his mother. Special agent Dobson sat on the edge of his chair and looked at the boy.

"How old are you, Chester?" he began.

"Thirteen," Chester responded.

"Do you know why I am here?" the agent continued.

Chester shook his head. "Not really."

"I have been tasked with assembling a team of people with paranormal abilities," he explained. "I have been given a small list of people to verify their abilities and return with them for a couple weeks of study. You, Chester, are at the top of my list. Do you remember the incident that your parents were just now telling me about?"

Chester nodded.

"Do you believe you moved that toy with your mind?" the agent inquired.

Chester paused, then shrugged.

Agent Dobson continued his investigation. "Have you tried transporting objects since then?"

"A lot," Chester said, feeling more at ease with the government official. "But mostly when I was younger."

"Were you successful?" Agent Dobson asked.

"Not even once," Chester confessed.

"What do you think happened that time with the toy?" Agent Dobson pursued.

"I don't even have a guess," Chester answered.

"When you were four, how did you think it happened?" Agent Dobson asked. "When I was four, I thought it was magic."

"You don't think that anymore?"

Chester just shrugged. He was too old to believe in magic, and if it were magic, why couldn't he do it again?

Ren took his badge from his pocket and tossed it to Chester. "Teleport it back to my pocket."

Chester closed his eyes, concentrated on the badge and the pocket. The other three watched in silence, all hoping Chester could do it, and believing he would, but the badge remained in his hand. He tossed it back to the agent, feeling a little embarrassed. He was less embarrassed that he had failed, more that he had tried.

"Let's take a look at that drawer!" Dobson said, standing up.

Chester's father, Mitchel, led the others to the master bedroom. Mitchel opened the drawer and the familiar scents filled Chester with memories. The agent removed the toy from the drawer.

"Is this it?" he asked as he handed it to Chester.

Chester took the toy from the agent's hand and nodded. He felt comfort in holding the beloved object.

"Send it to the drawer," Dobson instructed.

Chester closed his eyes and concentrated.

"Feel the excitement you felt that day when you were playing with it," Agent Dobson said softly. "You now hear your father in the hall and he's going to catch you with it."

Chester's mom gasped. Chester looked at her.

"Chester," she said, "look at your hands."

Chester looked, and the toy was gone. He turned his head toward the sock drawer. It was in the drawer, just like it was nine years ago. Ren handed him his badge.

"Feel the same excitement as you did when holding the toy. Now concentrate on the fear of hearing your father in the hall."

Chester concentrated on the same feelings, then opened his eyes. The badge remained in his hand.

Chester's face flushed red with anger. He struggled to hide the emotion in his voice.

His question came out as a whisper. "Why didn't it work? Why could I move the toy, but not the badge?"

The agent took the toy from the drawer again and handed it to Chester.

"Smell it," he instructed.

Chester put it to his face and smelled it.

"What does it smell like?" Dobson asked.

"Like everything else in the drawer," Chester replied.

The agent took the toy, put it into the drawer, and took out the whittled sticks. He handed the sticks to Chester, along with his badge.

"Move my badge back to my pocket."

Chester closed his eyes. The moment he thought of the badge being back in the pocket, he no longer felt the badge in his hand. He looked at the floor to see if he had dropped it.

"Chester," Agent Dobson exclaimed, pulling the badge from his pocket, "You did it!"

"How?" Chester asked, looking at his father. "Was it the smell?"

Mitchel slid one of the sticks from Chester's hand and smiled. "I made this when I was a boy," he chuckled. "I made magic wands. Maybe some of their power rubbed off onto the toy."

The agent said, "Mitchel, tell us about these wands."

"Back in grade school, I was one of the shortest kids in the class. I wished upon every shooting star, every birthday cake, just to be average height. One summer vacation I was hiking with the family and saw this stick on the ground."

He held up the wand. It was the crudest one, but it had a simple elegance to it. It was darker at the handle from a young boy's hand-sweat and dirt.

Mitchel continued, "I had long thought that there had to be some truth behind wizards and fairies using magic wands. I convinced myself that this was a magic wand in the rough. I took it home, sanded it to be uniform and smooth.

"All summer long, and into the sixth grade, I pointed the wand at myself, reciting made-up spells. I read every book on magic I could find. By the end of that year, I had caught up to some of the boys in my class and by the end of my seventh-grade year I was among the tallest."

"So, it worked," agent Dobson nodded, looking for Mitchel's confirmation.

"Maybe," answered Mitchel. "But both my parents were tall. I may have grown that much, anyway."

"Do you think it worked?" Dobson asked, looking for a more concrete answer.

Mitchel looked at Chester thoughtfully, then back at Dobson and confessed, "I did back then, and seeing what Chester has just done... yes, I think it worked."

Agent Dobson looked at Rosie and said, "I believe your husband crafted real magic wands. I need both him and Chester."

"You know," Chester's mom began, "I can..."

She was cut short by a child coming in from outside calling, "Mom, mom, mom!"

Rosie turned from the agent and took her daughter into another room to talk.

"Mitchel, get your books, wands, and anything you think might help," the agent urged. "Chester, we have everything you'll need at the base. Clothes, soap, toothbrush. You have just a couple of minutes to grab a couple of personal items to take with you."

Chester went to his room. He was so overwhelmed with conflicting emotions - fear and excitement, reluctance to leave home, but also eagerness for something new—that he just stood in the middle of his room processing it all. He soon returned to himself and looked around, wondering what he should take. He grabbed his wallet with three dollars in it, a book that he had been half-heartedly reading before bed, and he stuffed some hard candy into his pocket.

He went back to the family room where he waited in silence for his dad. His mom and sister came in and sat next to him. His sister chattered about her friend's new dog that she got to see today. Soon his dad came in with the agent and dropped his duffle bag to the floor. Rosie stood, walked to Mitchel, and embraced him. She then motioned for Chester to come to her. She kissed his forehead and told her daughter to say goodbye to daddy.

"He's going to visit an Army base for a couple of weeks."

Rosie grabbed Chester and hugged him longer than he was comfortable with, then let him go. He followed the agent and his dad out the front door. As they walked away from the house, the low sun cast their long shadows to the front porch, clinging to home until they entered the government car.

Chester stared out the window as they left the street, traveled out of town, and drove onto the freeway. The sun soon set. The motion of the car and the sighing sounds of cars passing soon lulled him to sleep.

Chapter 2

Chester awoke to the sound of boots on gravel, jogging in unison. He was momentarily surprised to find himself in a strange bed. He propped himself up on one arm and looked around. He vaguely remembered stumbling from the agent's car and flopping onto this cot. He did not remember the boy in the cot across from him, asleep in a tangle of blankets.

Almost the moment Chester looked at the boy, he awoke. It was an unnatural sight. A smile broke his face and his eyes opened as wide as a child's on Christmas morning.

He wrestled the covers that coiled about him until he was free, sat up, and said, "Good morning."

It was not that his voice was loud, but any voice shocks a normal brain like Chester's when it first wakes up.

Great, Chester thought. *A morning person.*

He didn't want to reply with "Good morning," because that would be a lie, but he did want to greet the guy.

"Welcome to... this place," he said, immediately feeling stupid for the awkward salutation. "I'm Chester, and that's my dad."

Chester pointed to the empty cot at the foot of his. "Yeah, he left over an hour ago," the boy said, standing up. "Let's get breakfast."

The boy looked to be about Chester's age, a bit shorter and solidly built. The boy headed for the door to find breakfast.

"Wait," said Chester. "Let me get dressed."

The boy said, "Don't you eat breakfast in your pajamas?"

"Yeah, at home," Chester answered, pulling jeans over his pajama bottoms.

He followed the boy out of the barracks into the compound. "Do you know where you're going... what's your name?" Chester asked.

"Orian," the boy said, scanning the buildings and people marching and hurrying about. He pointed to a short line of uniformed personnel. "That's the only line I see, so that must be the breakfast line."

Orian headed for the building and Chester followed. They crossed the road and could smell breakfast meats, breads, and maple syrup as they neared the building. Orian smiled and nodded at Chester and sped up to get in line.

Their excitement in finding breakfast quickly turned to fear when strong hands gripped their shoulders and spun them around.

Two muscle-bound soldiers leaned into their faces, one shouted, "This is a military base, what the hell are you doing here?"

Orian, with innocence and natural levity, pointed behind himself and said, "Breakfast!"

The same soldier's face became red with fury. He inhaled and screamed some more, "Breakfast? Why the hell do you think-"

The soldier cut his rant short and snapped to attention.

"What is this ruckus, Sergeant?" A voice commanded behind the boys.

The boys turned around and saw a Colonel addressing the angry soldiers.

"Two civilians on base, sir," the loud soldier said, his face still red from yelling.

"What were you going to do with them, besides yell?" the colonel asked.

The boys felt some satisfaction at the rebuke they perceived the soldiers were receiving.

The soldier replied, "Take them to the MP's, sir."

The colonel glared at the soldier, then said, "Well done, soldier. Make sure they are locked in a room together."

"What?" Orian gasped, looking at the colonel.

The colonel did not look at them. The angry soldiers gripped each boy by an arm and marched them to the MP's station. They were unloaded into a room with four chairs and a table in the middle. They looked at the door as it shut and then heard it lock.

Orian tried to open the door. Chester sat down and pointed to a chair across the table from him. "Make yourself at home."

Orian sat down and looked at Chester. "What is going on here?" he asked.

"I don't know," Chester answered. "That officer should have stood up for us."

"I know, right?" Orian said. "He's Colonel Fairmont. He recruited me!"

Chester tipped back onto the chair's back legs, trying to look relaxed, and said, "My dad will find us and straighten this all out."

To take Orian's mind off their current injustice, Chester asked, "What abilities brings you here?"

Orian looked at the locked door with indignation and huffed, "I can duplicate things."

14

"Like what?' Chester pursued.

Orian sat on the chair across the table from Chester. "Like rocks, pencils, coins, snowballs," Orian said. "In fact, a snowball was the first thing I ever duplicated. Once, during a snow day, the whole neighborhood was out having snowball fights. It somehow evolved from several small fights into a war between two streets on my block."

Chester listened closely as Orian smiled at the memory.

"My team was getting slammed, and I got separated from the others. Two older kids had me cornered against a fence and were pounding me with snowballs. In a panic, I chucked a snowball at one of their faces. The moment the snowball left my hand, it was two snowballs. I nailed them both in the face."

Orian chuckled.

"They both just stood there, surprised I guess, and a little freaked out. I was freaked out too, but I took off running and didn't stop until I was in my house."

"And you've been able to duplicate other things since then?" Chester asked.

"Yeah," Orian said, stretching across the table. "Give me a quarter."

Chester pulled a quarter from his coin pocket and dropped it into his hand. Orian did not close his hand or pass the other hand over it, another quarter just appeared in his hand, making a light clinking sound.

"Dang," Chester said. "I wish I had a twenty."

Orian nodded knowingly and placed the quarters on the table. "Give me your watch."

Chester obeyed. Just like the quarter, a duplicated watch appeared in his hand. "Look at it," Chester said handing the duplicate to Chester.

Chester quickly noticed that it did not feel like his watch. He turned it over and back.

Orian said, "It's like something from a cereal box, isn't it?"

"Kinda... but why?" Chester said, still studying the counterfeit watch.

"More complicated things don't copy as well. I've gotten a little better, but not much," he answered.

"How long... "Chester began another question when the door unlocked and opened. Colonel Fairmont came in.

"What's going on?" Orian demanded.

The two angry soldiers then entered the room. The boys stood in alarm and backed away.

"Hey!" Orian exclaimed.

The soldiers did not make eye contact and placed foil-wrapped breakfast burritos and some chocolate milk on the table.

"We apologize for our misunderstanding earlier," said the soldier who did the yelling earlier, then the two left the room.

Colonel Fairmont shut the door behind the soldiers and said, "Sit and eat and I'll tell you 'what's going on.'"

The boys sat back in their chairs and began to eat.

The Colonel said with some amusement in his voice, "I didn't figure two teenaged boys would rise so early and leave the barracks before we could talk. To get to the point, no one knows why you are here, and you are not to tell anyone. The personnel on this base were supposed to be told a cover story of why you are here, but that apparently has not yet happened. So, stay in your barracks until I say you can leave."

The boys nodded with mouths full. The colonel waited in silence as the boys finished their breakfast, then led them back to the barracks.

"Relax, play pool or video games," the colonel said. "The other two are getting settled and will join us for lunch."

The boys went to look for the rec room. It was not hard to find, being in the center of the building and the largest room. They played ping pong, fumbled around with the pool table, then played Zombie Blight on the gaming console until they were called for lunch.

They were escorted to a neighboring building into a classroom where lunch fixings were set out on a table in the back. Chester saw the back of the new peoples' heads. They were already seated and eating. Chester and Orian sat behind them, and Mitchel soon came in and sat next to Chester.

The person in front of Chester was an older woman with long silver hair, tucked neatly on the back of her head. The one in front of Orian was a girl, younger than the two boys, with a head full of dark curls.

Just as the boys began to eat, Colonel Fairmont went to the front of the room and spoke.

"The only people who know who you are and why you are here are in this room. Everyone else in this camp has been told that you are students interested in joining the armed forces someday, or adult supervisors of the students. Do not discuss any of your activities with anyone outside of those you see in this room."

The girls turned around and looked at the three boys and greeted them with a nod and a smile. Mitchel returned the greeting. The two boys tried to smile, but their mouths were full. The younger girl giggled at that and turned back around.

Colonel Fairmont took a step to the side and announced, "Special Agent Dobson."

Agent Dobson walked to the front.

"I'll make quick introductions, then you'll start with your training," he said. "Chester Thomas, come up here, please."

Chester stood up quickly, knocking his chair to the floor. Orian and the young girl chuckled. Chester's cheeks flushed with embarrassment as he walked to the front and faced the others.

Ren put a hand on his shoulder and said, "This is Chester, he can relocate objects."

Ren dropped his hand from Chester's shoulder and nudged him forward. Chester walked back to his seat, feeling deflated at the terse description of his ability. A bucket could relocate objects, after all.

"Orian Gruber," Ren said, motioning for Orian to come up front.

Orian stood and deliberately knocked his chair to the ground. Chester laughed loudly, quickly stifling it when no one else joined in.

"It was funny when Chester did it," Orian explained as he walked up and took his place beside the agent.

"Orian here can duplicate things," Dobson said, then nudged him forward too.

"Sandra O'Mally," Agent Dobson said with a warmth that was missing from the boys' introductions.

The older woman stood up and walked to the front. The hem of her dress rippled through the air as she walked.

"Sandra has the ability to stop objects that are in motion," he gave her a polite nod. "Thank you, Sandra."

Sandra took her seat.

Dobson smiled and called for, "Kwanele Sterling."

The girl energetically went to the front and smiled at the group. She was younger than Chester had first thought, ten or eleven at most.

He continued his introduction. "Kwanele here can change the path of a moving object. Large objects, if I understand correctly."

Kwanele looked up at him and nodded proudly. Ren thanked her, and she went back to her seat.

Last the agent called, "Mitchel Thomas."

Mitchel walked up to be introduced.

"This is Mitchel. Think of him as your quarter master and magic advisor. He has been studying magic since he was a boy and will be crafting your wands."

Kwanele bounced in her chair and clapped her hands quietly. Sandra leaned over and whispered something to her. Kwanele smiled and nodded.

Mitchel took a step forward and spoke.

"I need as much information about your abilities as you can give me to craft your wands. And if you have you have any suggestions or observations, please let me know. It will all help."

Agent Dobson raised his index finger in the air and said, "Weapons training in one hour."

Then he turned and left the classroom.

Mitchel took a chair from an empty table and dragged it to the girls' table opposite Kwanele. He took out a notepad and looked at her.

"What do you remember about the first time you used your power?" he inquired.

Orian tapped Chester's arm and motioned for him to follow. The two boys circled and sat next to Chester's dad.

Kwanele said, "I don't remember my first time."

"Why don't you remember?" he asked with his usual gentle demeanor.

"I was two," she answered. "My parents told me about it."

"What did they tell you?"

She told him that her apartment building was getting new air-conditioning units put on the roof. One day her mother took her outside and was talking with a friend. She was held by her mother, on her hip, as she talked.

"We heard a man shout from the roof," Kwanele said. "We looked up and saw an air-conditioner falling right above us. My mom said I went like this." Kwanele made a pushing movement with her hand. "It arched away from us and crushed on a parked car at the other side of the street."

"Wow," Chester exclaimed.

Mitchel wrote some things in his notebook. "Have you moved things since then?"

"Lots," she answered. "Once in school Mia's pencil rolled off her desk, and I made it roll under Evan's chair and she was too embarrassed to get it."

"She liked Evan?" Mitchel said with a knowing smiled. Kwanele laughed, "Yeah."

"Have you moved anything heavy like the air-conditioner since?" Mitchel inquired.

She shook her head.

"Have you tried?"

She nodded.

"When you moved the air-conditioner, were you holding anything, or was your mom wearing anything made of wood?" Mitchel asked.

"I don't remember."

"Did your mom have a wood necklace or pendant she liked to wear?"

She shrugged.

"That's ok," he said. "You have given me a lot to work with."

He turned to Sandra. "Tell me the first manifestation of your gift, Sandra."

"Have you ever wondered if you could make things move with your mind?" She asked, looking at each one at the table.

They all nodded.

"I have tried ever since I was wee. Even in my later years, I have tried. Just a year ago, I tried moving a metal bearing across a table. I did make it move... by tapping it with my finger. It rolled from the table and I reached out to catch it and it just stopped, in the air, between the table and my hand. In a moment or two, it fell again into my hand.

"I repeated the same thing over and over, and the bearing stopped every time. I have since tried, with success, stopping arrows and ping-pong balls. I've only done it for my amusement, though. I've found no practical use for it."

Chester's dad nodded and scrawled notes in his notebook. Chester watched Sandra until she looked in his direction. He tossed a grape at his dad's head. She subtly raised a finger on her left hand and the grape stopped dead, inches from his dad's face, and dropped down onto his notebook.

"See, no practical use for it," she said, winking at Chester.

Mitchel did not react to their antics. He finished his notes, stood, and left the room, flipping through the notebook as he went. Chester's eyes followed his dad as he left, and he thought he saw the two angry soldiers peering in a window then ducking out of sight. Chester said nothing of it and wondered if they saw what Sandra had done.

"Follow me to the shooting range," a new voice barked behind them.

"Why are we going to the shooting range?" Orian whispered to Chester.

"Because you are supposed to be finding out if you want to join when you are older," Sandra answered.

They stood, cleared their tables, and followed the soldier across the compound to the shooting range. Once there, they spent a long hour going over gun safety. Loading, handling, and "take care of your firearm and it will take care of you." Finally, they were ready to start shooting.

Orian was first to have his eye and ear protection on and was first to shoot. He was handed a pistol and told to load it and fire at his target. He loaded it with ease, pulled the slide back, released it, and started to shoot.

Both Kwanele and Chester noticed Sandra's finger flicking with each shot Orian took. Kwanele covered her mouth to conceal her laugh. Orian sat the pistol down, pulled off his ear protection, and looked at the Sergeant with confidence.

The soldier looked through his scope, then back at Orian. "The three bullets that hit the target were close together and near the center."

"I shot seven rounds!" Orian protested. "I've been shooting my whole life, how could I possibly-"

He cut his question short when he saw Sandra's smiling face and realized what had happened.

The others took their turns. Kwanele and Chester did better than Orian, while Sandra did better than all of them.

"Let me go again!" Orian pleaded with the Sergeant.

"You can all go again," he said. "Then we'll try the rifles."

They all reloaded and fired again.

"Very well, Orian, you did better than Sandra this time," the

Sargent said, looking through his scope.

They shot semiautomatic rifles with scopes, which Orian excelled at again. Finally, they got to shoot fully automatic rifles. Chester surprised the sergeant, Orian, and himself by being the most accurate.

The Sargent gathered the safety glasses and ear protection then remarked, "I have some real soldiers coming shortly. Are there any questions?"

"What do we do now?" Kwanele asked.

"Anything, as long as you're not on this shooting range," he answered.

They walked in the general direction of the barracks.

"Let's explore!" Kwanele suggested.

"You go ahead," said Sandra. "I'm going to lie down."

Sandra separated from the group, and the three kids went off to explore.

"Let's go to the exercise field and climb the tower," Chester suggested, and they pointed themselves in that direction.

On the way, they walked behind every building between them and the field. Behind some buildings there were crates, some marked with their contents, others marked with long strings of numbers and letters. Orian tried to open one of the coded crates until Chester place a hand on his shoulder and shook his head. Orian shrugged and continued toward the tower.

Behind the mess hall were the most crates, stacked well over their heads. They wedged themselves between the crates and came upon an open area. It was encircled by the crates stacked in steps, almost like a small arena. The three stopped before they entered the arena when they saw two soldiers at the other end, studying the contents of an open crate.

"It's them," Orian whispered.

"I saw them looking through our classroom window today," Chester said.

Kwanele asked, "Who are they?"

"Mean dudes," Orian said. "They tried to have us arrested."

The three kids watched silently. A few minutes later, the soldiers took a box from inside the crate and left through an alley between the containers.

Chester crept across the arena to the crate from which the soldier removed the box.

"Look," he said, pointing inside.

The others snuck across the clearing and peered in. There was a thin line of green and brown powder and some larger specks that had fallen through the slit on the bottom of the box the soldiers took.

Chester stuck his head in the crate.

"It smells like Christmas," he remarked, his voice muffled.

Chester took his head out of the box. Kwanele stuck her finger into the powder, then touched it to her tongue.

"Nutmeg and bay leaf," she noted. "And this red flake is rose petal. Why would they be cooking outside the mess hall?"

"And why be all secret about it?" Orian said.

"They may have seen Sandra do magic when they were looking in our window today," Chester said.

"What would cooking have to do with that?" Orian asked.

"What if they were making a potion?" Kwanele quizzed.

"Let's find my dad," Chester said. "He might know."

They squeezed through the crates the way they had come and walked to the center of the road. They looked up and down, but there was nothing to show them where his dad might be.

"Let's check our room," Chester suggested, and they ran to the barracks to find him.

They broke into the room, panting from their run.

"He's not here," Chester said.

Orian pointed to Mitchel's cot. "His books. Maybe there's something in them?"

They flipped through his books, looking for anything on potions.

"Here's one," Kwanele said, and began thumbing through the pages.

"See if there is an index in the back," Chester suggested.

Kwanele turned to the back of the book and found one.

"Bay leaf," she said and flipped forward through the pages. "It helps cure colds... attract fortune... protects from curses... and clairvoyance."

"Clairvoyance?" Orian asked.

"Seeing the future," Kwanele said. "Find nutmeg," Chester suggested.

Kwanele flipped through, found it, and read silently. "It's a lot like bay leaf."

"Rose petals," Chester said to her.

"Zuzu's petals. It's a Christmas potion," Orian said with a laugh.

"Rose petals," Kwanele said, pointing to the book. "Love potions, of course... healing bruises."

She looked up at the boys.

"And clairvoyance. They're trying to see the future."

"What's up with this place?" Orian asked. "Is everyone practicing magic?"

"I don't know." Answered Chester. "Everyone else seems to be regular army."

"I've been looking for you," Chester's dad's voice startled them. "Studying? I like that."

Chester felt a little embarrassed when Orian asked, "Mr. Thomas, did you ever make any potions?"

Mitchel sat down on his footlocker and answered, "No. This belongs to Chester's mother."

He pointed to the one Kwanele was holding.

"Do you know how to brew them?" Kwanele asked.

He answered, "From what I understand, they're not brewed in a boiling kettle. Rather, the ingredients are placed in a pouch, a handkerchief, or even a sock. Then you can wear it around your neck or sleep with it under your pillow. Chester's mom knows more about it than me."

Chester looked intensely at his dad and shook his head as covertly as he could.

Mitchel smiled at him and continued, "My wife has made potions and has tried making a sorcerer's stone."

"For turning lead into gold," Kwanele clarified.

"Yes," Mitchel acknowledged. "It can change many substances into others, but gold is usually the objective. Why are you wanting to make potions?"

"We're not," Chester replied. "We saw two soldiers making one."

"What exactly were they doing?"

"They were behind the mess hall mixing nutmeg, bay leaf, and rose petals," Chester said.

"I think you are all too caught up in your own mission that you're seeing magic where it isn't," Mitchel said.

"What else would they be doing?" Orian asked. "Cooking."

"With rose petals?"

Mitchel nodded. "Turkish delights are made with rose petals."

"Ew," Kwanele reacted.

Chester looked at her and nodded in agreement.

"But," Mitchel continued, "I do think that we are not the only secret this camp is keeping."

He smiled and pulled a thin pencil case from his back pocket and held it up. "Your wands. Let's find Sandra and try these out."

Chapter 3

Kwanele laid the book on the cot, and the four went to Sandra's room. She was not asleep but instead was on her phone telling a loved one that she was fine, and all would be okay.

Kwanele walked in and took Sandra's hand and pulled gently, "Wands, we got wands."

Sandra pocketed her phone, stood, and followed Kwanele. "The gym is reserved for our exclusive use for the week."

Mitchel said, leading the group out of the barracks.

He pointed at a building a hundred yards away. "The last building."

The kids took off running and Mitchel walked along with Sandra. When they reached the gym, the kids were chattered excitedly about trying out their wands. Mitchel punched in a code on the keypad and let them in. The building was empty. Their footsteps were annoyingly loud as they walked down the tiled hall, opened steel double doors, and entered onto a basketball court.

Other than two tables set up at one end of the court with different items on them, the court was empty. Mitchel opened the pencil case and pulled out an elegant wand of rich brown with a subtle purple grain in it.

"Oh," exclaimed Kwanele. "So pretty."

He handed it to Sandra, and she thanked him. He took out another wand. It was grey, the grain very straight, and at the end was a brilliant pink marquise-shaped stone. He handed this to Kwanele. She smiled and took it as if it were a fragile crystal.

"Thank you, Mr. Thomas," she said.

He gave Orian his wand next. White with off-white grain, elegant in its simplicity. Orian thanked him and started waving it around like a child with a lit sparkler.

"Thank you," he cheered.

Chester's wand had two kinds of wood joined side-by-side. One half had honey and red hues to it, the other half was black with gray tones. Chester thanked his dad and held it. It felt good in his hand, like a well-worn baseball glove.

"Let's talk a little about your wands," Mitchel said. "The wands themselves have no magic, but they help focus and amplify the magic put into it. Like a stereo speaker in a car, it can do nothing until a music signal is provided."

"Will we be using spells with them?" Orian questioned.

Mitchel replied, "Good question. The wands don't need them, but spells can help you quickly recall a feeling or pastime when you used magic. You'll choose what word or words you'll use. It is the same with how you wave your wand. You'll decide how to wave it to help you focus on the task you're trying to perform. Let's get started!"

Mitchel walked to the tables set up at the end of the ball court and the students followed. "I want to begin without the use of your wands, so put them on the table."

The students placed their wands on the table. Mitchel picked up a tennis ball from the table.

"Kwanele," he said as he wound up to throw the ball. "I'm going to throw this to the right of the backboard over there. When I do, I want you to make it hit the backboard."

He pitched the ball. Kwanele stuck out her arm and motioned her hand to the left. The ball moved to the left, and if Mitchel had thrown it hard enough, it would have hit. Orian snatched up another ball and threw it harder than Mitchel had. Kwanele waved her arm again, and the ball hit the backboard.

"Well done," Mitchel said.

Mitchel picked up another ball and tossed it to Orian. "Walk up to center court and throw it and try to hit the backboard this time."

As Orian made his way, Mitchel told Sandra to make the ball stop short, just short enough to make it drop into the basket. He gave Orian a nod, and he threw the ball.

Besides a hint of a smile, Sandra barely moved a finger. The ball stopped and fell into the basket.

"Well done," Mitchel said. He picked up another ball. "Orian, duplicate the ball after I throw it."

Orian nodded, and Mitchel threw the ball down the court. Orian opened his hand, but the ball did not replicate.

"I have to be touching it," explained Orian.

"I thought so," Mitchel said. "We are just creating a control or reference point and will go from there."

He picked up one more ball. "Chester, when I throw the ball, return it to my hand or the table."

He threw the ball. Chester instinctively made a grabbing motion for the ball. The ball continued its trajectory, landing on the floor, bouncing, then rolling to a stop. Chester turned his head a little from the others and shrugged.

Mitchel picked up a plastic cup and a feather from the table. He placed the cup on the floor, walked several feet away, and held the feather up, ready to drop it.

"Kwanele, when I drop this feather, move it to the cup."

He dropped the feather. As it floated, Kwanele thrust out her hand. The feather moved about an inch toward the cup, then continued floating downward. She thrust out her hand several more times and each time the feather fluttered toward the cup, then continued its downward path. It finally came to a rest just a few inches in front of Mitchel.

Kwanele looked puzzled. Chester felt discouraged that their strongest magician was failed by a feather. Mitchel picked up the feather and walked to the cup.

"This is all good," he said. "This is all good reference material."

He held the feather several feet in the air.

"Sandra, keep it from falling."

He released the feather. Sandra raised a finger. The feather paused in the air, then continued its descent. Sandra raised her finger with more intensity. The feather paused again, then continued falling. Sandra's calm face became serious and she raised both hands like Moses parting the Red Sea. The feather paused again for the same amount of time and fell again, settling on the floor next to the cup.

"Good," he said, looking at Sandra. "I got chills when you did this thing," raising his hands dramatically as she had. Orian nodded in agreement.

Mitchel picked up the feather and said, "Orian, concentrate. When I drop it, take your time and duplicate it before it hits the ground."

He dropped it. Orian concentrated and when he opened his hand, the feather suddenly puffed up to almost twice its size then hit the ground. Mitchel picked it up and showed it to Orian, then the others. The feather's shaft was split and now had two quills and nearly twice the barbs.

"Yes!" Orian exclaimed.

Mitchel looked at Chester. "Take your time and concentrate. When I drop it, return it to my hand."

Mitchel released it. Chester took a deep breath and concentrated. Halfway through the fall, he closed his eyes, and his clenched hand shook. He opened his eyes, and the feather lay on the floor. He felt more than disappointment. He felt shame for being the only one to have no success. For the first time in years, he felt like he might cry.

Mitchel recognized the look on his son's fallen countenance and quickly took Chester's wand from the table and pushed it into his clenched fist.

"Try it again," he spoke. "Remember the bomber."

He took up the feather and dropped it. Chester watched it fall, drew a breath, and pointed the wand at his father's hand. The feather vanished from its path and appeared between his father's fingers just as it was before it was dropped.

Success!

Chester breathed out with relief.

"Everyone grab your wands," Mitchel instructed.

They all got their wands and waited for the next exercise. Mitchel stepped away from the cup and held up the feather.

"Kwanele, let's try it again."

He let go of the feather. Kwanele tried different motions of the wand. Each time the feather moved forward a little then dropped. When the feather came down, it was further away from Mitchel than before, but still several feet from the cup.

"Why didn't the wand help?" she asked.

"It did," he said. "It is closer to the cup this time. Magic can come in bursts. The feather moved each time you told it to. The challenge for you is to keep the magic flowing. This time I want you to visualize filling the wand up with power the letting it out slowly. Like filling up a pitcher of water and letting it pour out."

He held the feather.

"Fill up the wand with power and let me know when to drop it."

Kwanele held her wand upright, concentrated on it, then looked at Mitchel and nodded. He dropped the feather. Kwanele let it fall a few inches, then she slowly tipped the wand forward. The

39

feather began to flutter toward the cup. She tipped the wand more and more, and the feather continued its steady path to the cup. When her wand was tipped all the way flat, the feather dropped just a few inches from the cup.

"Excellent!" Mitchel praised. "It will take some practice, but you have the idea. Now Sandra, keep the feather from falling using the same concept. Fill your wand and let me know when to let go."

Sandra took just a second to fill her wand and said, "Okay."

Mitchel let the feather fall. Sandra lifted her wand like a maestro, signaling the orchestra to get ready. The feather paused in the air for a good fifteen seconds, then fluttered down again.

"Nice job!" Mitchel said. "Now I want you girls to practice this together while I work with the boys. And I want you to picture yourself adding magic back into the wand as you pour the magic out."

The girls chose a couple of objects from the table and secluded themselves on the sidelines of the court to practice.

Mitchel looked at the boys and said, "Your practice will be a little different from the girls. It is the burst of magic that I want you to work on. Visualize the wand being filled with power, then release it all at once like a brilliant, one-shot roman candle."

He took another tennis ball from the table. "We're going to try the ball again. Orian, fill up your wand and tell me when to throw it."

Orian held his wand like a marine's sword in front of his face and said, "Ready."

Mitchel threw the ball down court. Orian stabbed the air with his wand toward the ball. There was a popping sound and two balls arched to the floor. One bounced like a tennis ball should, the other like it was somewhat deflated.

"Good work," Mitchel said, getting another ball ready to throw. "Again, with the ball, Chester. Store up the power and let me know when to throw."

Chester stood like a baton runner waiting for the starting gun.

"Okay!" he said.

Mitchel threw the ball. Chester thrust his want at the ball. The ball did not return to his dad's hand.

"Again!" Chester said.

Mitchel threw another ball down court. Chester stabbed at it again the ball was not returned.

"Again!" Chester said.

Mitchel walked over to his son and said quietly, "You'll get this, I promise. I don't want to put you on the spot here, but this is a perfect learning opportunity for everyone."

Chester said, "Yeah. Sure."

Mitchel called for everyone to come over for a minute. "Orian asked about spells earlier and now is a good time to try one out. Chester is going to think of a spell to help him return the ball to me."

Mitchel turned to Chester. "Think back to when you were four, and you made that bombing scope return to my drawer. Remember how you felt physically, and emotionally. Recall any sounds or smells."

Smell! That's what he remembered most. The smell of that sock drawer. He closed his eyes and thought of the smell, the fear of disappointing his dad, the sound of him in the hall, and the sigh of relief when the toy was gone.

"Breathe!" Chester said, opening his eyes. "'Breathe' will be my spell."

"Ready?" Mitchel asked.

"Yes!" Chester said with new confidence.

Mitchel threw the ball down court. Chester pointed the wand at his father's hand and whispered, "Breathe."

"Excellent!" Mitchel said, holding the ball for Chester to see.

It had returned. He finally transported a moving object.

"Can I go next?" Kwanele asked excitedly.

"Yes," Mitchel said, tossing the ball to Chester. "When you were making the feather move toward the cup, what were you feeling or thinking?"

"I was pouring magic out of the wand," she answered.

"And when it was empty, the feather fell?" Mitchel quizzed.

Kwanele nodded.

"I think your spell should be for filling up your wand as you are dumping it out," Mitchel said. "What spell would you like to use to fill your wand?"

Kwanele twisted the corner of her mouth and looked up as she thought.

"Glub?" she said, unsure of her choice.

"Glub. I like that. Let's try it out," Mitchel encouraged and stepped ten feet from a cup he had placed on the floor. He held Orian's mutant feather up and asked, "Are you ready?"

She looked at her wand and said, "Glub... Okay."

Mitchel let the feather go. Kwanele tipped her wand, and the feather moved steadily toward the cup.

"Glub," she said and tilted her wand up and began tipping it forward.

When her wand was halfway down, she said, "Glub."

And lifted it upright again. The feather made it all the way and came to rest in the cup.

Kwanele jumped and clapped her hands.

"Good job," Sandra said, putting an arm around her.

"I'm guessing you're ready, Sandra?" Mitchel asked.

"Ready," she answered.

Mitchel held out his hand and said, "Chester," then motioned for him to throw the ball.

Chester tossed him the ball.

Mitchel held it up and said, "When you're ready."

Sandra kept her arms to her side and chanted, "Loading, loading, loading," then nodded to Mitchel.

Mitchel let go of the ball. Sandra held up her wand, and the ball stopped.

She chanted again but only slower, "Loading... loading."

The ball hung in the air for a full minute then slowly slipped down then dropped. Kwanele jumped and clapped, just as proud of Sandra as she was of herself.

"Nicely done, Sandra," Mitchel said.

Mitchel walked to the cup and took out the malformed feather, "You're up, Orian. Just tell me when."

Orian took his time thinking up his spell.

At last, he looked at Mitchel and said, "Okay."

Mitchel let it go. It fluttered a bit.

"Splat!" Orian shouted as he pointed his wand at the feather.

Two identical mutant feathers floated to the ground.

"Hey, hey!" Mitchel said, picking the feathers up showing them.

Orian held his wand in the air and faced Chester.

"High wand!" he shouted excitedly.

Chester raised his wand and tapped it to Orian's. Orian went to the others for a "high wand" and they cheerfully obliged.

Mitchel raised his hand and announced. "We have a couple of hours to work on this. Chester and Orian, work on your skills. Think of your weaknesses and work on those. Sandra and Kwanele, let's talk."

The boys took a box of different items from a table and went to the far end of the court. Mitchel approached the girls.

"Both of your magic is in the movement of matter, but only matter that is already in motion. I have specific plans for all of us, and yours' require moving an object that is at rest."

He pulled a ball bearing from his pocket and placed it on the floor.

"Looks familiar," Sandra mused.

Mitchel said, "I don't know how to tell you to make it roll, but try."

The girls spent ten exhausting minutes waving their wands, shouting spells, and making gestures that would make a mime laugh. Mitchel stood there the whole time, studying them with a hand over his mouth and eyebrows pressing low over his eyes.

Mitchel took his hand from his mouth and said, "Let's try something else. I told the boys to load their wands, then let it all out with a single burst. Try that."

He took a step back and put his hand to his mouth again and watched. The girls loaded their wands and pointed their wands, and the ball bearing remained unmoved.

This went on for another ten minutes or so, until suddenly Sandra said, "Wait, I have an idea."

She bent over and poked the bearing with her wand.

"Ta-da."

Kwanele laughed, and Mitchel rose his eyebrows for just a moment.

"Kidding aside, I do have an idea," she said. "Load your wand, honey, and on three we will try to make it move together... One, two, three!"

They pointed their wands and commanded, "Move!" in unison.

It wasn't much, but the bearing spun. It spun slowly and only a couple of times but it did move.

Mitchel got an idea. The girls could see it on his face.

"Clean up!" he hollered across the court. "I have some research to do."

In a couple of minutes, all the gear was back on the table and they all went outside.

As Mitchel locked the door, he told the students, "We are going on a field trip tomorrow. Go to the barracks, have some dinner. Rest and play some games. Do not, I'll say it again, do *not* practice your magic. We can't have anyone learning about us."

Mitchel hurried off in one direction, while the students took their time going back to the barracks. Once there they played, ate, rested, and went to bed early, all mentally exhausted from their training.

Chapter 4

The next morning, they took an army truck on a field trip. They drove a half-hour to a vast cratered field. Mitchel got out and unlocked the gate, then they drove in. There were the burned-out remains of tanks, armored vehicles, and busses scattered everywhere. They drove to the end of the dirt road and gathered behind the truck.

Mitchel let down the tailgate, reached in, and pulled out two staffs. One was about five feet long, the other about four. He walked out into the field and climbed up on a large flat slab of concrete that had smaller chunks of it all about. He set the bottom of the larger staff on the slab. It was straight, cylindrical, and tapered slightly near the bottom. There was a place near the top and another a foot lower where the staff narrowed.

Mitchel pointed to the lower of the two and said, "Kwanele, hold the staff here with your left hand."

She stepped up and took hold.

"Sandra," he continued, pointing to the upper narrowing. "Hold here with your right hand."

She took hold of if it as instructed.

Mitchel said, "I'll give you a minute to load the staff with magic, then I want you to work together to lift that tank."

He pointed to a heap of metal that used to be a tank fifty yards away.

Sandra nodded rhythmically as she whispered, "Loading, loading, loading."

Kwanele stood motionless, eyes closed in concentration. There was not a sound. It seemed as if the wind and the locusts were waiting, breathless, to see what was going to happen, just like the three guys.

Are you ready?" Sandra asked Kwanele.

"Yeah."

They lifted the staff.

"Up," Sandra commanded softly.

"Up!" confirmed Kwanele.

"Up," they said in unison.

The sound of metal being stressed was heard and dust shuttered from the tank. The tank lifted off the ground. It didn't look like more than a couple of inches, but it was definitely in the air.

"Woo-hoo!" Chester said.

"Hold it there as long as you can," Mitchel instructed.

A couple of seconds later, the tank dropped with a metallic crunch and a plume of dust enveloped it.

"Yes! Excellent!" Mitchel said. "Keep practicing. Lift it higher, hold it longer. Lift more than one thing at a time. I'm going to help the others and I'll be back."

He pointed off to the left of the group and said, "Chester, go out there, away from all this noise. Find something alive to transport. Grasshoppers, chipmunks, lizards, anything. You will need to be able to transport people, without injury. I'll catch up with you later too."

Mitchel motioned Orian to follow. "I have some things in the back of the truck for you."

Mitchel and Orian walked back to the truck, and Chester jogged to a quieter place to practice. He kept going until the thunderous sounds of heavy armor crashing to the earth was just a distant thump. He slowed down and walked quietly through the yellow grasses and brush, looking for any living thing larger than a fly.

He did not see anything on any plant or on the ground. He found a boulder to climb up on and sit. He waited quietly, listening, and looking for any movement. It was not long before a chipmunk scurried by and halted near a hole in dry earth just a few feet in front of him.

He slowly pointed his wand at the chipmunk and whispered, "Breathe."

It worked, kind of. The rodent was gone, but where did it go? He looked all around his stony perch and saw no sign of it. *I can't be sending people off to some random place,* he thought. *I have to tell it where to go.*

He pointed at a fist-sized rock with his wand and pointed his left finger to the chipmunk's hole in the ground.

"Breathe," he whispered.

The rock was transferred and covered the hole. He looked around for another creature to move. The chipmunk found its way to its hole and began to remove the rock.

He pointed his wand at the chipmunk and his left finger to the foot of the boulder he was on.

"Breathe."

The chipmunk appeared at the foot of his stony perch. It pawed at the air like it was just pawing at the rock over his hole. It sniffed and scurried back to the rock over its home. Chester pointed at the rock and his empty finger to a clearing twenty yards away.

"Breathe," and the rock was gone from the rodent's entrance and rested in the clearing. The chipmunk scurried into his home.

He waited for quite a while for something else to appear, and nothing did. He stood on top of his boulder and looked around. At last, he saw movement in the distance. He could not tell what it was, but he could see its back appear above the grass, then disappear and reappear as it ran. He pointed his wand at it and his other finger to the foot of the rock.

"Breathe," he yelled loud enough for the creature to hear.

There was a flurry of fur and dust at his feet as the animal continued its sprint. It moved so fast and there was so much dust that he could not quite tell what it was, but by the reddish fur, he assumed it was a fox.

He was feeling confident, but he needed to know if he was hurting the animals. The furry ones got away too quickly, so he got off his rock to look for locusts or grasshoppers. He walked slowly through the taller grass, hoping to scare an insect into the air. He did not find a locust or grasshopper at first, but he did stubble upon a busy anthill.

He could start with an ant, he supposed. He held his wand but did not point it. He just concentrated on one ant and his opened hand and said, "Breathe."

The ant appeared in his hand and did not squirm or twitch the way an injured ant does. It just walked on like nothing had happened. He looked at it closely to make sure it had all its legs and antennae. It looked fine.

He wondered if he could move more than one ant at a time.

He circled the wand over the hill and said, "Breath."

This was not his best idea. Ants covered his hand and started up his arm. He quickly brushed them off and backed away from the hill.

He walked back to where the others were to report to his dad what he had done. When he was close, he stopped and watched the havoc the girls were creating. They were doing something new. They both had staffs now. They would load both up with magic, each would take their own staff and cast an individual spell.

Sandra was holding vehicles high in the air and Kwanele was throwing others several hundred feet. She would squeal with joy each time one violently crashed to the earth.

Chester smiled at the fun they were having. He looked down at his arm, at the red welts the ants left.

"I can move ants," he mumbled sheepishly to himself.

He headed to the truck. Orian and his dad were still at work when he arrived. There were dead potato bugs and snails all over the truck bed and tailgate. There were several empty jars and a few more with more test subjects crawling over each other.

Orian had a live snail on the tailgate in front of him. Chester watched silently. Orian muttered a spell as he circled his wand around and around it. He stopped his chant and the circling. There were two snails now in front of him. Orian groaned in exasperation.

"Wait, wait," Mitchel said, staring at the snails. "Look!"

He poked one snail in the eye with his finger. The eye retracted, then slowly extended out again.

"You did it," he said, happy and relieved. "You did it."

Chester walked up and said, "Wow! That's more complex than a watch."

"Yeah," Orian said, exhausted.

"How did you do it?"

"I store power in my wand like the girls do and concentrate on duplicating it from the inside out," Orian said, pointing to all the failed remains. "'Til just now it's been a gooey disaster. How's it going with you?"

"I'll show you," he replied.

He looked around for a critter to transport. He felt the vibration of a heavy vehicle crashing to the earth, then the sound of Kwanele's happy squeal. He realized that anything alive was either hiding or has fled.

"Hold out your hand," he said to Orian. He pointed his wand at the two snails that Orian had just copied and said, "Breathe."

Both appeared in Orian's hand. Orian stroked their shells like little pets. Mitchel lifted one from Orian's hand and inspected it.

"It looks fine. Have you tried this with any mammals?"

"A chipmunk and a fox," he answered, trying to hide his pride from Orian who still looked a little discouraged.

"Any damage done to them?" Mitchel asked.

"They were too fast for a good look," Chester answered. "Not damaged enough that they couldn't run, at least."

"We'll need to take one with us to observe over the next couple of days," Mitchel said. "I have to be sure that you will be okay when you transport people."

Chester had not really thought about any damage being done to people, but he began to worry about it now.

"Will you make me a staff?" he asked his dad.

"No," Mitchel responded with a sharpness that he did not intend. "The girls need them because they need more power and more amplification to do what they will need to. You need precision, and from what I've seen, you have it."

"You keep saying that we'll need to do this or that, I thought we were just being studied for a couple of weeks. Why would I have to move people and Kwanele need to throw tanks?" Chester pressed his father for details.

Mitchel ignored the question, put the snail in a jar, and put on a lid. He wiped his hand on his pant leg and whistled to get the girls' attention.

He waved for the girls to come back. "Time for lunch."

He looked at the mess of dead insects all over the back of the truck. "Do you think you can clean this off?"

Chester nodded. He waved his wand over the tailgate and pointed to the ground several yards away. All the mess on the tailgate was removed. He repeated the process to clean off the truck bed.

Mitchel climbed in and pushed two coolers and some blankets to the tailgate. He hopped out and took one cooler to a nearby tree. Chester handed the blankets to Orian and took the other cooler.

They spread out the blankets under the tree and opened the coolers. One was filled with ice and drinks, the other had sandwiches, chips, cookies, and fried chicken. When the girls arrived, they were smiling and chatting about the fun they were having.

Kwanele took a soda, opened it, and said," We're going to need bigger stuff to throw around." She took a drink.

"There is something much bigger," Mitchel said.

"Where?" she asked, looking around.

"Eat, then I'll show you," he said. "I want you all to be there for it."

"Why do they need to move anything bigger than a tank dad?" Chester urged for an answer.

Mitchel looked at the team members, they all looked back with anticipation. He told them, "We are not here to be studied, our government wants us to back up our troops on a battle against some terrorists."

"Who?" Sandra quizzed.

"I haven't been told everything yet," he admitted. "I am told that we will be there in a supporting role only, but we will not go if we don't all feel ready."

They continued with their lunch. Terrorists were on all their minds, but no one spoke of it. Chester asked to see Kwanele's staff. She handed it to him proudly. It looked much like her wand, but it had a different stone embedded in the top. It was a rough and ordinary-looking stone, and it surprised him that it was not polished or translucent or glowing.

It had a good balance. He stood up with it and stepped away from the others. He wound up like it was a baseball bat and pointed to the imaginary bleachers, imitating the famous Babe

Ruth moment. He looked out to where he was pointing and saw a vehicle rapidly approaching, stretching a dust trail behind.

He handed the staff back to Kwanele.

"Dad, someone's coming!"

Mitchel stood and looked to where Chester was pointing. "This place is off-limits," he said. "It may be Fairmont or Dobson but hide your staffs and wands under the blankets just in case."

They stowed their staffs and wands under the blankets and tried to look like they were just out for a relaxing picnic. Soon the vehicle was in the clearing where their truck was. As it approached, Chester and Orian recognized the occupants of the truck. Their hearts pounded in their chest.

It was the angry soldiers.

The truck stopped a few yards from them. The one on the passenger side jumped out and the other drove off.

The passenger pointed to Chester and said, "We know what you're up to, Chester. You'd better get ready!"

The passenger ran several paces away from the group, faced the road where his driver was turning back around. The passenger closed his eyes and held his arms out like wings. The truck's tires were spitting dirt and gravel as it gained traction and headed straight for the soldier.

"Chester, get your wand!" his dad urged, pointing to the blanket where it was hidden.

Chester started, "But Kwanele and Sandra-"

Sandra cut his sentence short. "Have never moved something living. Do it, Chester."

Chester threw back the blanket and grabbed his wand. The truck was seconds from striking the soldier down.

"Breathe," he said, pointing to the ground to his left.

The soldier appeared on Chester's left-hand side. He swayed and put his hands on his knees. Mitchel ran over to him and stood him back up.

"Are you alright? Are you hurt?"

He put out his arms again, said, "Ha ha!" then put his arms down. "That was intense! And a little painful. But I feel fine!"

Mitchel felt the soldier's head and arms and walked around him, inspecting him. "How many fingers am I holding up?"

"Three."

"What is your name?"

"I don't remember," the soldier said, shaking his head to revive his memory.

Mitchel ran his hands through his hair nervously.

"Kidding! Just kidding," the soldier quickly said. "Private Bates. Private Rand Bates."

Mitchel relaxed a bit, then smiled a half-smile. He shook the soldier's hand. "Who told you about Chester?"

The soldier walked to the cooler and took out a soda. "Chester did."

Mitchel gave Chester a disappointed look. Chester shook his head, his eyes wide with innocence.

"When I grabbed him to take him to the brig," Bates began.

He took another soda out and threw it to the other solder who was now joining us.

"I saw him, in my head, standing in a battlefield, then the image was gone."

Private bates pointed to the other soldier. "I told Corporal Da Silva here about it, and he said that his grandmother had similar premonitions."

Corporal Da Silva continued the story. "She used to mix herbs and things to help her conjure seer-dreams. I e-mailed my mother for her recipes."

Kwanele interrupted, "Rose pedals, nutmeg, and bay leaf!"

"Yes," Corporal Da Silva said. "Among others, but nutmeg and bay leaf were all we could find in the kitchen."

Bates took it from there. "I've been putting a small bag of it under my pillow every night since. I dreamed of you all fighting someone I could not identify. Early this morning I saw Chester, and I could feel his conflict over transporting a human and worry about hurting them. We came here to force him to transport a human and get over his fear."

Corporal Da Silva finished his drink and motioned to Bates that they needed to go.

"If anyone asks, we were never here," he said, looking at the group.

"Wait!" Said Mitchel as they turned to leave. "What else did you see?"

"Nothing that made sense to me, and nothing else about you guys." The private said. "It's all kind of new to me."

The soldiers went to their truck and drove away. Mitchel turned to his students.

"Clean up," he said. "We have a lot more to do."

Chester said, "I'll clean up and catch up to you in a minute."

The others walked toward the concrete slab where they first stood this morning. Chester put a garbage bag in his left hand

and with his wand in his right, he began transporting the garbage to the bag.

He heard Orian behind him say "Splat," and his used plate and soda can was doubled.

"Breathe," said Chester, pointing to the drink cooler to transport it right at Orian's feet.

Orian stumbled over it and laughed as Mitchel helped him back to his feet.

After the garbage was collected, he folded the blankets, placed them on a cooler, and transported both coolers and blankets to the truck.

He looked at the others walking to the field of destruction. He held his wand to his chest. He did not say "breathe" out loud but thought it, and as he did, he thought of transporting himself to the cement slab.

His thoughts froze. He felt intense fear and pain all over, like sparks emanating from his bones. As quickly as these sensations came, they were gone, and he was standing on the concrete slab.

"Chester!" Mitchel scolded as they all arrived at the slab. "Do you feel all right?"

"It did hurt," he chuckled. "But not as much as walking all the way."

Chester held up his wand for Orian who gave him a high wand. Kwanele looked around.

"I don't see anything bigger out here," she noted.

Mitchel told the girls to hold Sandra's staff and load it. "Focus your lift ten feet underground, below that tank, and lift the earth under it like a column."

They heard him. They knew what he was telling them, but they just stood there, looking out at the field. Mitchel waited patiently. The girls turned to each other and discussed what to do.

They chanted as they filled the staff, then they lifted it. Dirt, rocks, weeds, and probably an animal or two flew high into the air, leaving a diminishing trail of dust behind. A few seconds later it all began to fall back to the earth with prolonged percussions.

The hailstorm of rock and dirt created more dust as it pounded the ground.

"Not like that, I guess," Kwanele smirked.

Mitchel answered, "No, but that was a good start."

He fanned the dust with his hands.

"And can someone get rid of this dust?"

Chester readied his wand, but Sandra was already passing her staff over the field. The dust peeled away like a curtain, getting thicker as it got shoved aside. The dust settled slowly, far out to the right, leaving their stage clear for another violent production.

"Let's dig deeper and raise it real slow," Sandra instructed Kwanele.

They reloaded the staff and raised it slowly. The ground shook. Rocks and pebbles bounced on the vibrating ground. A low-pitched grinding sound rumbled in their chests. A ring of dust blew into the air around the tank. The tank rose slowly on a mound of earth.

The mound became a pillar, rising slowly.

As the pillar lifted, rock and dirt broke away from it. More and more fell from the pillar, and the tank slid off to one side. After rising fifteen feet or so, it looked more like a cone than a pillar.

They put the staff back to the ground. Sandra leaned on it and breathed heavily. Chester asked her if she was alright. She said she was, and that she just needed to learn to breathe when she was using magic.

Mitchel encouraged them, "Keep practicing. Do some really wide ones and see how high you can raise them. Orian, Chester, *walk* back to the truck with me."

Back at the truck, Mitchel pulled out two folded wire cages.

"Orian, stay here. You are doing well and now I need you to be able to copy those snails quickly."

He handed Chester a cage.

"Now let's go catch a fox."

They made the long walk back to the boulder Chester was at earlier. He climbed to the top and looked around for a fox. Mitchel set up the cages and looked around.

Several minutes passed without any movement.

"Doesn't need to be foxes," Mitchel said. "Rabbits or lizards will do."

After a long while, Mitchel climbed the rock and searched with Chester.

"This is worse than fishing," Chester said, bringing his arm down from shading his eyes. "At least with fishing you can cast and reel in and bait the hook. This is torture."

Mitchel looked at his watch. "It hasn't even been an hour yet."

At last, there was movement in the distant grass. Chester quickly pointed his wand at the target and his left finger to the cage. Without having to utter his spell, there was a sudden flurry of red fur in the cage.

"You got a fox!" Mitchel said. "Now see if you can catch one more animal."

They searched for nearly an hour more with no luck, and the fox was looking hot and thirsty, so Mitchel called off the search and said, "Go get Orian, but don't-"

Chester transported himself before his dad could tell him not to. He thought it would hurt less the second time, but it did not. When he appeared back at the truck to get Orian, he panicked a little when he saw two trucks. Orian was sitting on the tailgate of one.

"Who's here?" he whispered.

Orian hopped to the ground. "No one," he said. "Doesn't it look familiar?"

Chester looked at it. Aside from the open tailgate, they looked identical.

"You copied the truck?" Chester asked.

"Yep," Orian answered and went to the driver's side of the new truck and climbed in. Chester followed and got into the passenger side.

"Watch," Orian said.

Orian turned the key, and the truck started up. He revved the engine several times, then turned it off.

"Perfect copy," he said with a smile.

"It is!" Chester acknowledged, touching the seat and dashboard. "Come on, my dad wants to see you."

They got out of the truck and Orian began walking.

"Want to try transporting there?" Chester asked, twirling his wand.

"Doesn't it hurt?"

"A little, and only for an instant."

After a pause, Orian agreed. Chester circled his wand once around them both, and they were back with Mitchel.

"Ow," Orian groaned. "But better than walking."

Mitchel crouched by the fox's cage talking cutesy to it.

"He's sleeping in your room, and you have to walk him." Chester joked.

"Orian. How is it going with the snails?" Mitchel asked.

"Great. And they have a brand-new truck to play on."

Mitchel did not understand and didn't want to. He pointed to the cage. "Duplicate the fox and try to keep the new one in the cage."

Orian pointed his wand at the fox and said, "Splat."

"Splat" sounded wrong to Chester for duplicating an animal, but it worked. The new fox yelped. Both foxes looked at each other, barked, and began to scuffle.

"Chester, transport them together into the other cage," Mitchel said.

There were two yelps from the other cage where they continued to bite and tumble, unaware that they had been moved.

"Again," Mitchel said.

Chester pointed his wand and finger, and they were back to the first cage, continuing their battle.

"Okay," Said Mitchel. "Put them in separate cages."

Chester moved one to the empty cage. They both continued fighting for a moment, then stopped at the same time and looked around confused that the other was not with him.

"No more transporting humans until I've had a chance to observe these guys for a negative reaction," Mitchel told Chester. "Can you transport them to the truck for me?"

Chester circled his wand.

"Wait!" Mitchel interrupted. "Transport them back to the barracks."

Chester closed his eyes and pictured the barracks in his mind. "Breathe," he said, circling the foxes with his wand.

He could still hear the foxes panting in their cages. He tried it several more times with no luck.

"I think I have to be able to see the destination to do it," he sighed.

"Work on that," Mitchel said. "In the meantime, transport them back to the truck. We'll get the girls and head back."

Chester sent the furry cargo to the truck, and they walked to get the girls.

"I guess Sandra can drive the other truck?" Orian said, wanting acknowledgment of his latest triumph.

"What other truck?" Mitchel asked.

"I got bored with snails and duplicated our truck," Orian said.

"And it works?" Mitchel asked.

"Perfectly."

"How fast did you do it?"

"Quick as a fox," Orian answered, and ran the rest of the way, followed closely by Chester.

They looked at the new land formations the girls had been working on. There were a lot of crumbling cones of differing sizes, some pillars, and several buttes of impressive heights.

"Nice work," Mitchel complimented when he arrived. "Time to head back." "Yeah, okay," Kwanele answered.

"Do you want to transport back with me?"

Kwanele nodded excitedly and Sandra said, "I sure would."

"No, Chester, dang it!" Mitchel exclaimed.

Chester circled his wand and transported the five of them to the trucks.

"Ouch," said Kwanele, followed quickly by, "Oh, cute," when she saw the foxes.

Mitchel walked around the new truck, touching it as he went.

"We can't go back in two trucks..." he looked at the front bumper, "...with the same license plates without people getting curious."

"We can't leave it here without someone getting curious either," Chester observed.

Mitchel interrupted Kwanele who was talking to the foxes. "Kwanele, would you mind putting this truck out there," he pointed to her practice field.

She stood, loaded her staff, and swung it like a fishing pole. "Yah-hoo!" she yelled as she hurled the truck.

"Yesss," she congratulated herself when it landed and tumbled, then burst into flames.

"Load the foxes into the truck. We need to get back," Mitchel said.

"Can I ride in the back with them?" Kwanele asked, lifting one cage into the truck.

"I need you all in the cab. We need to talk," he answered.

When the foxes were stowed, the students climbed into the cab and they drove off. Chester knew what his dad wanted to talk about and started the conversation.

"I know we don't know the long-term effects of teleporting, but it is a risk we have to take now, not later."

Mitchel silently looked out the windshield as he drove. It was apparent that he was holding back emotion. Chester had never made him that angry before, but he didn't feel bad for it. He was in the right! A tear flowed down Mitchel's cheek and he quickly wiped it away. Okay, now Chester felt a little sorry.

"That's not what I wanted to talk about," Mitchel said, forcing his emotions down. "I just wanted to let you know how proud I am of you all. You have all exceeded my expectations."

Mitchel's phone chimed. He quickly pulled over and took his phone from his pocket. Everyone was quiet while he read.

"I just got a text from Colonel Fairmont. Terrorists have taken prisoners. We leave tomorrow, and what was to be a mission to wipe them out has been changed to a rescue mission first... then we wipe them out."

"Are we ready?" Kwanele asked.

Mitchel smiled a spontaneous smile, "They won't even know what hit them."

Chapter 5

"Let the foxes go," Mitchel said, putting the truck in park. "We won't learn anything from them now."

They all went to the back of the truck, took out the cages, and set them on the ground. Orian opened one cage and let out the fox. It took a couple of timid steps forward, then scurried off.

Kwanele opened the other cage.

"Go on," she told it.

It too took a couple of trepid steps and ran off in the same direction as the first.

They put away the cages and drove to camp. Mitchel dropped the others off at the barracks while he and Chester parked the truck.

"We'll have dinner in the classroom in one hour," Mitchel instructed.

After the truck was parked Mitchel suggested that Chester

transport them back to the barracks. Chester circled his wand and transported them.

Arriving in the barracks Mitchel, stretched out the sting and said, "You like doing that, don't you?"

"Yeah," Chester admitted. "A lot."

"I'm going to shower before dinner," Mitchel said.

A shower sounded good to Chester, so he got his towel and soap and took his time in the spray. As he relaxed under the hot water, he thought about how his powers would not be effective in fighting. Sandra's and Kwanele's roles seemed obvious.

He nodded to himself when he realized that his dad had a plan for each of them. That put him more at ease, and he finished his shower. He got dressed and joined the others for dinner. Orian was seated with his dinner and was unusually quiet. Chester figured that he was thinking the same thing about his powers, wondering how they could be useful in a fight.

Chester tried to lighten his mood, well, both of their moods, by transporting Orian's steak to the other side of his tray when he went to stab it. Orian retaliated by doubling and then doubling again the peas on Chester's tray.

"Hey," Chester groaned.

Then Orian upped the ante by doubling his brownie. They both laughed.

Kwanele looked at Orian and pointed to her brownie and uttered, "Hmmm?"

Orian happily doubled her brownie, too.

"That has some real peacetime potential," Chester said.

"Peacetime, yeah, but I don't know what good I'll be in battle," he said quietly so that only Chester could hear.

"I feel the same way," Chester admitted. "But my dad as a plan for all of us. He sees our value."

As they finished their meals, Colonel Fairmont turned on the flatscreen at the front of the class and spoke.

"We know where the terrorists are encamped, and we have footage of them. You need to see we are up against. This is the first footage we have of them caught on security cameras at a gas station about two hours from here."

He pointed a remote at the screen and started the video. The recording was low quality and details unclear, but it was clear enough to discern six figures enter the station, all dressed in the same drapery clothes. They passed out of view of the camera. A few moments later a few plastic pop bottles slid across the floor toward the door, followed by the six figures with what seemed to be an unconscious or dead man and a woman draped in the arms of two of them. He stopped the video.

The Colonel looked at the class, but mostly at Kwanele, "Remember, you are supporting our troops and will be out of harm's way."

He resumed the video.

"A similar encounter was happening at a weapons depot not too far from the gas station."

Ten individuals dressed in the same fashion as those in the first video marched toward the gate of the weapons depot. One of the four guards at the gate ordered them to halt several times. When they failed to yield, the four guards opened fire.

They could see the clothes of the ten pressing against their bodies when the bullets hit and puffs of dust behind them where the bullets impacted the earth.

"The bullets pass right through them like they're ghosts!" Sandra gasped, failing to hide the alarm in her voice.

The terrorists breached the gate, grabbed, and subdued the soldiers in a matter of seconds, and dragged them from the depot. The colonel stopped the recording.

"Finally, this is from a helmet-cam of one member of a special ops team who tracked down a small group of them."

The Colonel resumed the video. The footage was dizzying. Bouncing and turning left and right as the men ducked through tall grass and brush. The backs of other soldiers and flashes of their boots occasionally appeared through the vegetation.

Gunfire and shouting began. The soldier with the helmet-cam stood up. There were two terrorists twenty-five yards in front of him. He fired his weapon, cutting down the grass with rapid-fire. They moved toward the soldier. They seemed to be slowed by the gunfire but not stopped by it. Another must have come up from behind him because the camera fell from his head and hit the ground. The remainder of the footage was a still image of grass and the rapid lessening of shouts and gunfire until there was dead silence.

The colonel finally spoke. "Thousands of rounds of ammunition were fired, a dozen grenades employed. Nothing stopped them. Our conventional weapons are of no use. We need something beyond the conventional. We need you."

Colonel Fairmont turned off the TV and quietly left. Mitchel told them to leave their plates and suggested an early bedtime to be ready for a busy day. The boys and the girls went their own ways and got ready for bed.

It was twilight out when they settled into their cots. Chester stared out the window at the orange sky. He was excited to use his magic and to be with his new friends, but still worried about his contribution.

His father's voice broke the silence, addressing both boys. "You know, a sniper's role is just as important as a tank's. Oh, by the way, Bates and Da Silva will be joining us. Now get some sleep."

Chester's sleep was broken, and he woke before Orian and his dad. He showered quickly, got dressed, and went to the rec room.

He sat and stared at a black TV screen, letting random thoughts enter his mind and leave without entertaining any.

"Chester, will you help us?" a voice sounded behind him.

Chester turned and saw Private Bates and Corporal Da Silva standing in full combat gear. He quickly got up, eager to be active. He followed them outside to an armored Hummer and cargo truck.

"Help us move all these boxes and crates into the truck," Da Silva said.

Chester could have just transported it all, but he wanted to do something normal for a change. He helped Corporal Da Silva carry cargo to Private Bates, who stood in the truck to move and stack it all.

Corporal Da Silva said, "I guess you heard that we're coming with you."

Chester nodded. "It will be good to have some foresight."

Private Bates said, "That, and Da Silva here is an explosives expert."

"Have you ever teleported explosives?" asked Bates. "You'd better make sure you can. What I felt when you transported me seemed like it could ignite an explosive."

Bates hopped out of the truck, took his sidearm from its holster, removed the clip, and pushed a bullet out. He placed the bullet on the ground.

He looked around, pointed to rock outside the campus, and said, "Let's all back up, then move that bullet to that rock over there."

They all backed away from the bullet. Chester pointed to the bullet and the rock. The bullet transported. There was a moment of silence, then a *pop* and a *za-zing* out in the field. They turned toward the rock. A puff of dust lingered where the bullet fired.

"You would have leveled half the camp if you did that to one of those crates," Da Silva said, pointing to the crates they had left to load.

"Let me try another," Chester insisted.

Bates slid another out of his magazine onto the ground. Chester thought about trying to move it slowly. He concentrated on a slow transport, pointed at the bullet and its destination. They heard a pop and zing from the field.

"One more," Chester said, walking toward Bates with his hand out.

Bates slid a bullet into Chester's hand. Chester kept the bullet in his hand, pointed to the rock, and transported. No explosion, no ricochet.

"Do you have a grenade?"

"What?" exclaimed Da Silva.

"We have to know," said Chester, holding out his hand.

Da Silva handed him a grenade. He held it in an open hand and transported it to the field. No explosion. He saw it perched on the rock. He pointed his wand at it and his finger farther out in the field. Smoke, rock, and dust flew all around where he transported the grenade, then they heard the boom.

Chester grabbed Bates' arm and transported him to the bed of the truck.

"Did that hurt?" Chester asked.

Bates shook his head. "No. Didn't feel a thing."

Chester ran to a crate with explosives in it. He placed his hand on it and transported it out to where the grenade exploded. No explosion.

"I can do it if I touch it!" he said, then transported himself out to the field.

He put his hand on the crate and transported it to the truck. He then appeared back at the explosives that needed loading and transported them each into the truck.

"Now that's done, we have a short briefing in your barracks, then we leave," Bates said, jumping from the truck, and they headed to the barracks.

At the barracks, bagels, muffins, and juice were laid out.

"Where have you been, Chester?" his father asked as the three came in. "We're about to start."

Chester pointed to the other two. "Helping them load the truck."

Chester and his 'angry soldiers' fixed themselves a plate and sat down. Once everyone was settled at a table with their breakfast, Mitchel and Colonel Fairmont went up front and addressed them.

Colonel Fairmont spoke first. "Mr. Thomas is in charge of this mission. You will do everything he says. If he cannot perform his duty, Ms. O'Mally will be in charge."

Mitchel spoke next. "Right now, there is little activity around their camp. We will survey it from a distance, see if Chester can extract the hostages, then assist the troops in destroying them. Get yourselves in the Hummer, it's about a two-hour drive from here."

Everyone stood. The soldiers were first out the door, then the girls, then Mitchel. The boys lingered to collect snacks from the breakfast table, then made their way to the waiting trucks. The soldiers got into the cargo truck and the rest got into the Hummer.

When all were seated, Mitchel turned in the driver's seat to look at them and said, "Everyone, show me your wands."

Everyone showed him they had them. He nodded, turned around, and started the engine. They followed the supply truck out of the camp and onto the smooth paved road. The girls chatted while the boys ate and stared out their windows.

Chapter 6

After nearly two hours, their vehicle pulled off the smooth pavement onto a dirt road. Chester was suddenly alert with the knowledge that they will be fighting an actual battle. His stomach was filled with butterflies, much like he felt his first time up-to-bat as a young little-league baseball player. He looked at the others. Orian just looked annoyed to be off the smooth road, Sandra was hard to read as she leaned forward to look out the front window, and Kwanele was her usual excited self.

The ride got rougher and slower as the road became less of a road and more of a foot trail. After a few bumpy minutes, the vehicles came to a stop.

"Uh-oh," said Mitchel. "Bates looks worried."

Mitchel rolled down his window as Private Bates approached.

"Our scouts say they've spotted us," he said. "I thought we would get a lot closer than this, but they are already in vehicles and headed this way. The troops are waiting for us to signal that we have the prisoners. We don't have much time."

"Thanks, Private." Mitchel acknowledged, then turned to his students. "This is it. Keep calm, listen to instructions, and we'll get through this. Grab your wands and let's go."

They all quickly got out of the Hummer and gathered around Mitchel.

He pointed to the field left of the trucks, "Sandra, Kwanele, we need a two-hundred-foot-high plateau as a look-out point."

The girls stepped through the high grass a hundred yards out. Sandra spread her arms, the staff in her right hand. Kwanele put her hand on the other end. In a few moments, the ground on which they stood began to rumble and rise. A breeze caught Sandra's long gray hair and green dress, blowing them behind her, giving her a look of a grand wizard as they rose on their huge plateau.

The guys stumbled and knelt on the shaking ground until the plateau came to a rest. Rocks and earth sloughed off and tumbled down the face and to the ground.

Mitchel stood and said, "Chester, get the crates up there, and us."

Chester hopped into the back of the truck, touched a crate, and sent it up on the bluff. He transported each crate to the top.

Then he said, "Everyone, grab a hand."

He reached out and grabbed his father's hand. Mitchel took

85

Orian's, and the two soldiers joined in.

Chester whispered, "Breathe," and all were relocated to the top.

The soldiers pried open a crate. Bates took a pair of binoculars, ran to the edge of the cliff, and looked out.

"Mitchel!" he hollered and motioned for him to come.

Mitchel ran to Private Bates and took the binoculars.

"How were they able to build tall buildings out here in such a short time?" Bates quizzed.

Mitchel did not answer and pressed, "Do you have stronger glasses?"

Bates ran off and returned with Da Silva lugging a crate. They quickly removed a tripod and binoculars three times the size. They mounted them to the tripod and Mitchel looked.

"Those aren't buildings," his voice trembled. "They look like missiles, very large missiles."

Bates took a turn looking through the binoculars. "Okay. It all makes sense to me now. All the dreams that I couldn't understand!" he related.

He moved the binoculars. "Look at their transport."

Mitchel looked.

"See," Bates continued. "No wheels. It looks like the legs of a centipede, and those aren't missiles, they're spaceships. The terrorists are aliens!"

"Kwanele!" Mitchel hollered, waving his arms for her to come.

She ran to him, staff in hand. "See those busses heading toward us?"

Mitchel asked, pointing down at the approaching transports.

Kwanele nodded. Mitchel instructed her to throw them up into the air as high as she can.

She pointed her staff at a vehicle on the right and sent it skyward with a shout of "Wee-hoooo!"

The transport slowly rotated end over end as it rose high enough that Sandra and the boys saw it hang at its highest point and begin its fall. They ran over to watch what Kwanele was doing.

The alien transport hit the ground, tearing apart as it rolled to a stop. Kwanele sent another soaring.

"Sandra," Mitchel instructed. "Help her destroy the other three transports."

Kwanele sent a third one into the air before the second landed. Sandra lifted the fourth and held it about one hundred feet in the air. She directed her staff downward, smashing the transport on top of the last one.

"Well done!" Mitchel complimented. "Now, we need to get closer to find the hostages. Sandra and Kwanele, make us another plateau halfway between us and those buildings in the distance."

Sandra and Kwanele took ahold of Sandra's staff, paused, then raised it slowly. The ground shook. Chester watched pebbles and rocks bounce on the vibrating ground, then out to the field where a new earthen pillar was rising. When it was complete, Michele began directing their next move.

"Bates, Da Silva, do you have what you need?"

They acknowledged in the affirmative.

"Chester, your up! Everyone, come together!" he ordered.

"Chester, put us up there," he continued his commands as he pointed to the top of the new lookout.

Chester grabbed Orian's arm. The others took another's hand or arm, and Chester moved them to the new summit.

Mitchel pointed to Bates and commanded, "Find where those prisoners are held."

Private Bates poured out some powder from a zip-lock bag and rubbed it on his face. He sat down on the ground and closed his eyes.

"Dad!" Chester shouted. "What's going on? Those aren't

buildings, they're missiles or something."

"It doesn't matter, Da Silva and Bates will be going in, not you or the others," Mitchel stressed.

Chester looked at Da Silva who was looking at the ships with binoculars. Chester pointed his wand at Da Silva and transported the binoculars into his hand.

"Chester, wait!" Mitchel demanded.

Chester immediately moved himself to the edge of their new stage and looked at the missiles and the terrorists below them. He searched the plateau for Sandra, found her, and transported her to his side. He handed her the binoculars and pointed to the ships and the activity below. She surveyed the scene, then lowered the glasses in astonishment. Chester took her hand and transported them back to Mitchel.

"Aliens, Dad, aliens! Were you not going to tell us?" Chester interrogated.

"We are here for support. I didn't think it mattered," Mitchel explained. "I only found out myself after we got here."

Mitchel looked at Bates, who was just beginning to stand.

"Did you see them? Do you know where they are?" Mitchel pleaded.

Bates nodded and pointed, "Second from the left."

"Call it in," Mitchel instructed. "Send in the troops and tell them to stay clear of the ships. Chester, move the rest of us to the ledge."

Bates put a satellite phone to his ear and Chester moved himself, Sandra, and his dad to where Orian and Kwanele waited. They all grabbed a hand and were transported to the edge of the plateau.

Chester pointed to the ships and terrorists and announced, "Those are spaceships, and those are aliens!"

Sandra handed the field glasses to Kwanele.

She looked out and exclaimed, "Cool!"

She handed the glasses to Orian to have a look. He looked forward, then panned to the right.

"We're engaging!"

The others looked to the right. Five thousand foot soldiers and thirty tanks began to attack. They saw muzzle flashes, explosions, then heard faint sounds of battle. The aliens surged toward the army.

"We're not stopping many of them!" Orian narrated the scene.

Sandra put her hand on Chester's shoulder. "Get a big boulder up here as fast as you can."

"There's a jar in my pack on the first plateau," Mitchel interjected. "Put a bee or wasp or anything that stings in it and bring it to me, but the rock first."

Chester nodded and disappeared. In a moment, a boulder the size of a dump truck appeared a hundred yards behind the group. A couple of minutes later Chester appeared with a jar containing several black and yellow hornets.

"Orian!" Mitchel called. "You're up to bat!"

Orian handed the binoculars to Mitchel. "Duplicate that boulder. Make fifty." Mitchel instructed. "Then duplicate this jar of hornets, as many as you can."

Mitchel looked out onto the battlefield as Orian duplicated boulders with a heavy thump of each. The army outnumbered the aliens four to one, but the aliens were not stopping, many of them had reached the tanks. The aliens piled themselves under a tank, one upon the other, and slowly lifted the front of the tank up and flipping it onto its back.

He heard Sandra call Kwanele's name. A moment later he saw the first duplicated boulder plow into the sea of aliens. It appeared to have squashed and killed several of them. He put down the glasses and watched as Kwanele sent another boulder soaring towards the enemy, then crash into the crowd.

They all began to hear a new sound from the battle below, a reverberating sound like large sheets of metal being flexed. The aliens were firing weapons at the soldiers. Bright silvery projectiles zipped through the air from the rear of the alien hoard toward the army. Shortly they were beginning to fire up at the Sandra and Kwanele.

Some of them were now headed toward their plateau. Bates grabbed Mitchel's arm and looked at him in a panic.

"You have to send me and Da Silva now, they're gonna kill the hostages."

Bates took out his pistol, ejected the clip, examined it, then slid it back in.

"That will do you no good," Mitchel explained. "Chester! Get me a gun from one of those aliens."

Chester peered over the ledge, then shook his head. "I can't see their guns, we're too far away."

"Bring one alien up, then take his gun," Mitchel suggested.

Chester gave a wry smile and pointed his wand at the rear of the alien troops. An alien appeared before him that twitched a moment in pain. Chester transported the weapon from its hands to the feet of Bates. The alien stood bewildered, starring at Chester. Its eyes were little more than horizontal slits, but they were a fantastic glacier-blue color. Kwanele shouted, "Aaaarrr," as she swung her staff toward the alien. It was swiftly hurled backward, off the plateau, landing with a violent tumble to the feet of its comrades. She rejoined Sandra in mashing the foe with stones.

Mitchel called for Orian, who had now created hundreds of duplicate jars of hornets.

"Duplicate this gun," he instructed, pointing at the weapon at Bates's feet.

Orian complied. Bates took up the guns, handed one to Da Silva. "Chester, put us on that ship, second from the left."

Chester circled his wand, Bates, Da Silva, Orian, and he vanished from Mitchel. Mitchel's heart sank.

"Chester! No! Chester!"

The four boys appeared before the girls, then all six disappeared.

"Damnit, Chester! You're not a soldier!" Mitchel screamed.

Chapter 7

Sandra and her team were teleported to a large room in the alien ship that had a hundred chairs with harnesses. The chairs were arranged in a spiraling circle, like seeds in a sunflower.

Private Bates pointed his weapon all around the room.

"No one's here," he said quietly.

"They're all out there," Sandra whispered, pointing behind her. "Can you see where the prisoners are?"

He handed his gun to Orian and poured more powder into his hand. He pocketed the remaining powder, rubbed his hands together, and then rubbed his face.

"I see them," he said with his eyes close. "They're well-guarded, but seem to be alright."

"Can you see how we can get to them?" Sandra asked.

Bates concentrated. He turned his head, then his body. Lifted his head and lowered it as if he was looking up and down a stairwell. He turned his head side-to-side then nodded.

He opened his eyes and said, "Follow me."

As they followed Private Bates inside the quiet ship, Mitchel was busy running to the stockpile of insect-filled glass jars, grabbing them, running to the plateau edge, and hurling them down on the heads of the aliens who had begun scaling the cliffs. The shattering glass was as much of a deterrent as the insects themselves, causing some aliens to lose their focus and fall.

"They're going to reach us in a few minutes," Mitchel thought. "They'll need to rescue them soon."

The rescue was not progressing as fast as anyone wanted. Sandra and her team were growing nervous. Every moment aboard the ship was another moment closer to a violent encounter, and they no longer had the home-court advantage.

They came upon a closed door.

Bates looked at the door. "How does it open?"

There was no knob or handle, no button to push. He waved his hands around to activate any motion sensor. Nothing happened.

"The paint is kind of dirty there," Da Silva noticed and touched that smudged area of the door.

The door slid open with a hiss, exposing a ramp that seemed

to spiral from the base of the ship to the top. They entered the ramp-well and began to ascend. They passed a couple of doors as they climbed when they heard the hiss of a door above them open. They froze. Bates slowly pointed his gun up the spiral.

They stood silently while the footsteps and talking of two aliens grew nearer. The talking was melodic and sounded like a language consisting of mostly vowels. Sandra's team waited in silence for the aliens to come around the bend. The aliens didn't expect the humans at all and didn't have time to react before Sandra sent them flying upward, smashing into the ramp above, then falling limp before them.

The noise echoed up and down the ramp-well.

"More will be coming now," said Bates.

They hurried up the ramp, skirting the lifeless alien pair to the door the aliens had just used.

"This should be the level they are on," Bates said as he opened the door.

He and Da Sliva peered out the door. It was just a hallway with no aliens to be seen. They walked down a hall and turned down another.

"We're close," Bates said.

They turned down another hall, where they startled a group of aliens walking toward them. Bates and Da Silva got off a couple of shots, blowing holes through several aliens. Kwanele shoved the rest back with incredible force, smashing them against a wall in a room at the end of the hall. She kept them pressed against the wall until they stopped squirming, then let them drop.

"Hello?" a voice called from the room, followed by several cries for help.

Sandra's group ran down the hall to the room. forty or more men and women were up against a wall, restrained at the waist.

Sandra said, "Private, keep an eye out for incoming aliens. Chester, transport them to the hill."

Chester said, "I can only transport to somewhere I can see." "Bates," she bellowed, "What direction is the hill?"

Bates pointed in the direction he faced. "Kwanele, punch a hole in this wall."

Kwanele took a step back, loaded her staff, and pointed it at the wall.

The wall concaved quickly with a loud groaning. Then a hole tore through.

"Keep punching until you can see outside," Da Silva told her.

The next wall groaned as Kwanele punched a hole through it.

97

"Enemy approaching!" Bates shouted, squaring his stance for battle.

"Keep punching," Sandra said to Kwanele. "We'll take care of the aliens."

Kwanele punched another hole in another wall, and the private and Corporal began firing on incoming enemies. The ship was not built with onboard battle in mind. The halls were just wide enough for two alien soldiers to charge side by side. It was easy for Bates and Da Silva to pick them off as they came down the corridor.

Kwanele punched a hole in the last wall.

"I'm through," she called.

Chester looked through the holes. He saw the plateau in the distance. The cliffs were covered with climbing aliens.

"They're halfway to the top. I can't transport them into danger," he pondered, pointing to the prisoners.

Bates explained, "There's no less danger on this ship!"

Chester pointed to the plateau he saw through the hole in the ship and circled his wand around the prisoners.

"Breathe," he said, and the prisoners were gone.

"Are there more onboard?" Sandra asked Bates.

"I can't see. I need a moment to concentrate."

Sandra walked to the doorway and pointed her staff down the hall where dead aliens were strewn, ready to take care of any more aliens. Bates held some of his concoction to his face and closed his eyes.

He nodded. "Yes, one more, a child. It's in a room with only two guards, but there are a lot more aliens in a big room between the ramp and the child. They seem to be waiting for us. Probably every remaining alien on board. Most of them are dressed differently than the ones we have seen. I don't think those are soldiers. This way."

The team followed Bates back to the ramp and ascended. They passed two doors, then stopped at a third.

He spoke. "This opens up to a big room where they're waiting for us. I sense a lot of fear among the civilian aliens."

Kwanele asked, "What are civilians?"

"Aliens who aren't soldiers," Bates answered.

"I don't want to hurt any of them!" Kwanele protested. "They're scared!"

Bates thought a moment. "Okay, we can use their fear. Kwanele can you tear a big gash in the door?"

Kwanele nodded.

"Okay," Bates continued. "When I say go, tear a hole in the door, then Chester can transport us to the hall just behind them. Once in the hall Sandra, I'll need you to bring down the ceiling or bring in the walls to keep them from following. Ready? Go."

Kwanele drew her staff across the door. A crack formed in it with a loud pop, then crunching of metal as it pealed apart. Panic gripped the civilian aliens, and they fled from the humans, running into the soldier aliens, making it impossible for them to shoot with any accuracy.

Chester circled his wand and transported them to the hall behind the frenzied alien mob. There were several civilian aliens in the hall running away from them. Sandra lowered the top of her staff at the opening of the hall, bringing down part of the ceiling. Metal, wire, and other debris fell in a mass blocking any aliens from pursuing.

They ran down the corridor, behind Bates, to a room where a child in a hoodie was bound and an alien soldier to either side. The aliens raised their weapons and were quickly shot by Bates and Da Silva.

"Which way to the plateau?" Sandra asked Bates.

He pointed. Kwanele knocked out a hole in the wall. She was pushing out another wall when a loud crash came from above them, followed by dust and debris falling all around them.

Before they could figure out what was happening, they were surrounded by alien soldiers. Surprise was on the alien's side this time, and they yanked the wands and the guns out of the human's hands.

"Ow!" Orian shouted, holding his right hand in his left.

The aliens pressed the humans against the wall. They felt pressure around their legs that bound them to the wall. The aliens stepped back and made room for another alien to enter.

This one had to be a superior. His robe was fashioned in the same manner as the soldiers', but it was hunter-green with orange sleeves. His raiment had more embellishments, as well. As he walked past the others, they handed him the wands and guns.

The superior glared at the six new prisoners, then at their weapons. He held the weapons in front of him and paraded them in front of the prisoners, talking loudly. There was a harshness in the melodic language. He dashed the weapons to the floor in a dramatic gesture and leaned toward Sandra, shouting with increased intensity.

He raised his fist and swung at her. Sandra flicked a finger, halting his fist just inches from her face. He swung his other fist at her. Again, she halted the blow. He curled his lips back from his teeth, held out his hand toward the soldiers. One soldier meekly picked up one of the guns and put it into the leader's hand.

"Chester," Orian whispered. "Chester."

Chester looked. Orian pointed to the palm of his hand. It was swollen and bleeding. Chester shook his head, not understanding why Orian was showing him this. Orian pointed at the source of the blood. The tip of a large splinter was sticking out.

Chester nodded as he understood that a large splinter of Orian's wand had stuck in his hand when the alien stripped it from him. Orian held out his bleeding hand toward the leader, who was pointing the gun at Sandra and still ranting.

"Splat!" Orian shouted.

Everyone turned to look at him. The leader pointed his gun at Orian.

"No!" Sandra shouted, holding her hands out toward the alien leader.

At that moment, the leader was knocked to the floor. Sandra looked at her hands, surprised for a moment that she could have done that without her staff. She gasped when she saw what had knocked the leader to the floor. A second leader, exactly like the first.

"What have you done?" she asked Orian in horror.

Chester said, smiling wryly. "Oh yeah! The foxes!"

The leader who was knocked to the floor got up and shoved his clone backward. He pointed his gun again at Sandra. The clone wrapped his arms around the original, and they violently wrestled around until the original was free from his clone's grip.

They sized each other up, grabbed each other, and rolled around on the floor again, shouting at each other. The soldiers backed away from the brawl in fear and confusion.

Kwanele focused on her staff muttering, "Come on... Come on."

She held her breath when the scuffle came close to their wands and sighed when the fight moved away. Again, they rolled toward the wands, and one of the aliens kicked Chester's wand. It was kicked away from the prisoners, but it was in motion, so Kwanele was able to divert the direction it was rolling toward Chester. There wasn't enough momentum to move the wand close enough for Chester to reach.

The conflict escalated, and the two leaders began to punch and claw at each other. A solid hit knocked one backward, and he kicked Kwanele's staff with enough force that she was able to guide it to her feet. She bent over, stretched as far as she could, and picked up her staff.

"Hey, ugly and ugly!" She shouted to the leaders.

They paid no attention. Orian and Chester joined Kwanele in shouting at them for their attention with no success. Private Bates put two fingers in his mouth and made a shrill whistle, and they stopped.

Kwanele smiled broadly and waved her staff. "Look what I got!"

Both leaders reached for the same gun on the floor, but before they picked it up Kwanele lifted them and pressed them against the opposing wall, and kept pressing. Their forms flattened some under the pressure. They squirmed with pain for a few seconds, then were still. She let them fall to the floor with a loud slap, then restored the wands and guns to their owners.

Chester transported himself and then each team member out of their restraints, but kept the child captive still, insuring they all stayed together.

"They're coming back to their ships!" Bates said, staring blankly at a wall. "All of them."

"Which way to the plateau," Chester demanded.

Da Silva pointed, and the Kwanele burst holes through the walls with a single blow.

Chester pointed his wand at the child and his finger at the plateau. The child was transported.

He gathered the team together, looked outside to the plateau, and said, "Breathe."

Chapter 8

Back on the plateau, Chester hardly had a moment to collect his thoughts when he was grabbed by a familiar grip on his shoulders and was turned around. His father looked at him with anger which evaporated quickly to pride then back to his commander's face.

"Bates, call the troops back," Mitchel ordered.

Bates made the call, then Mitchel pointed toward the aliens. "Take those ships out!"

Several of the ships were already beginning to take off, leaving hundreds of their kind behind. Sandra was first to act. She pointed her staff at the one ship that was in the air. She drew her staff downward. The bottom half of the ship tore away from the top, then blew apart in a brilliant orange blast.

Kwanele made the same motion, which tore a wide gash in the side of another ship in flight. A ball of fire gushed from the gash, followed by the entire thing exploding with thunderous noise. Sandra lifted the prisoner ship slowly into the air, several hundred feet above another grounded ship, and let it drop, crushing the other ship in a prolonged rumble.

Chester pointed his wand at a crate of munitions left on their first staging area, and his finger to another ship in flight.

"Breathe!" he shouted.

The crate disappeared from the plateau, then the munitions exploded inside the nose of another ship in flight. The ship pitched to the left and arched to the earth in flames, exploding on impact.

Orian enjoyed watching the ships being taken down one by one, but he couldn't help feeling a little jealous of the abilities of his friends. Chester knew Orian's feelings and went to him.

Chester said, "Remember the feathers we trained with?"

Orian nodded.

"Remember the Siamese feather you created?"

He nodded again.

Chester pointed to a ship just taking off. Orian, with showy flare, pointed his wand.

"Splat!" He shouted.

The ship's twin appeared, conjoined at the top. The thrust of the two ships completed, spinning them slowly until they slopped side-to-side, tearing each other apart.

Orian shouted, "Yeah!" when it blew in two fiery bursts.

He pointed to another ship just lifting off. He made Siamese quadruplets out of it, joined at the top in a semi-circle. It spun like a giant firework, then each ship slammed in succession against the earth.

"Let the girls finish off the ships. We'll take care of the guys they left behind," Chester said.

Chester vanished and, in a moment, returned with a munitions crate beside him. "Make twenty copies."

"Okay," Orian nodded.

When they were copied Chester explained, "If I transport explosives without touching it, it will explode at its destination."

Chester took Orian to the edge of the cliff and pointed to the front of a crowd of aliens running to the last couple of ships on the ground.

"There!" he said. "When I teleport it down, duplicate the explosion?"

"Okay," Orian replied, pointing his wand to the same spot.

Chester pointed his wand at a crate and said, "Breathe."

A bright blast sent many aliens flying.

"Splat!" Orian said a fraction of a second later.

Another blast appeared near it, sending another group of aliens sprawling.

Da Silva and Bates showed up beside the boys, firing at any alien separating themselves from the crowd.

"Ready?" Chester said. "Same place... Breathe!"

Another fireball sent aliens asunder, quickly followed by Orian's which appeared in a denser part of the mob. Mitchel, the girls, and several of the liberated captives joined them at the edge, cheering with each discharge.

"There's still so many!" Orian observed.

Kwanele raised her staff, lifted one of the two remaining ships, and held it high above the alien swarm. She let it drop and tore a gash into it just before it impacted. Fire swelled through the tear, then blew up.

"Splat!" Orian said with finality, and two identical flaming ships engulfed most of the crowd.

Sandra stood by quietly, then said to Kwanele, "I did the first, you do the last."

Kwanele imitated Sandra's Moses-parting-the-Red-Sea stance,

raised the last ship over the now dispersing aliens, and let it fall, splitting it open before impact. Orian duplicated it before it exploded, a few hundred yards away, to trap the last fleeing aliens. Two enormous flashes of flame covered the field, then a low *boom, boom* shook the ground.

Everyone on the plateau surveyed the plain all around. Flame and smoke covered much of the battlefront. Da Silva searched for any signs of alien activity. He spotted a few survivors that he pointed out to Bates to take care of.

Mitchel took out his phone and called Special Agent Dobson.

"It's done," he said.

"How many people did you rescue?" Dobson asked.

He counted the number of people rescued and said, "Forty-nine."

"Are you sure?" Ren asked. "Our intel showed forty-eight."

"Hold on," Mitchel said, and started a recount.

He stopped his count when saw one survivor with a hoodie, standing apart from the others. He seemed to be a child, short and slender, his clothes too big for him, and he kept his head down and his hood around his face. Mitchel walked over to him and pulled back the hood.

"Yep, you're right." He told Agent Dobson. "There are just forty-eight."

"Good work," Ren said. "I'll be sending choppers out to pick all of you up, so sit tight."

"See you soon then," Mitchel ended the call.

He looked at the top of the boy's head, who still looked down. It was covered with a wispy kind of feather. Mitchel knelt in front of him and lifted his chin. His whole face had the same wispy feather texture, but not as much as on his head. His face was human enough, but his beautiful coffee brown eyes were larger than a human's.

Kwanele saw the child and ran over. She plopped a pack on the ground in front of her, squatted, and opened it. She pulled out two granola bars and opened them. She took a bite of one and handed the other to the child. He gracefully took it from her and smiled, showing his ruby-like teeth.

"Oh," Kwanele said. "She's so pretty."

"Yeah," said Mitchel. "Could be a girl. Go get Chester and Bates for me, please."

Kwanele got up, and in a moment returned with Chester and Bates.

"Oh!" Chester startled, seeing the being.

Mitchel gravely looked at Chester. "I need you to get her out of here before the FBI arrives."

"Okay," Chester said.

"Private, take them to my house. And I need you to tell no one about our new friend here," Mitchel said.

"Yes sir," Bates said.

"Oh, and take Kwanele with you. I think the child be more comfortable with her around," Mitchel added.

Kwanele zipped up the pack, put it on, and took her new friend's hand. Chester took the other, put a hand on Bate's shoulder, and transported back to the supply truck and Hummer.

Chester got up front with Private Bates, while Kwanele, and the child got into the back.

"Call your mom, let her know where you're going and that you're okay," Chester said, looking back at Kwanele.

"Can I tell her about Kimmi?" she asked, pointing to her new friend.

"I'm telling my mom about her," Chester said.

They heard helicopters approaching as Bates started the Hummer and turned it around. Soon, two chinook and two cobra choppers flew overhead toward the plateau. Chester rolled down his window, stuck his head out, and watched until they landed.

He rolled the window back up, closed his eyes, and fell asleep.

On the plateau, Agent Dobson wrote down the names of each person as they got onto the choppers.

"Where's your boy and the other two?" he asked Mitchel after everyone else was on board.

Mitchel answered, "Kwanele wasn't feeling well. I had them take her to my home for my wife to take care of until her mother can be sent for."

Ren nodded, then looked around at the smoking landscape.

"They performed as well as I hoped, and better than I ever expected. I'll drop everyone off at the base and fly you and the rest of your team home."

"Okay," Mitchel said and climbed aboard.

Chapter 9

It was a short trip to the base, and the survivors were led away to be checked out by the base physicians. Mitchel looked out the window to the other chopper where Sandra and Orian were being lifted to their homes. He waved, and they waved back.

"I'll get off here," Agent Dobson said, to Mitchel's relief.

The agent was about to stand, then held up his finger and reached into his suit coat pocket for his phone.

"Hello, Rose," he answered, giving Mitchel a puzzled look. "Yes, that would be great! I'll set that up right now."

He hung up the phone.

"You're going to detour to pick up Kwanele's family. Rose wants them to be there when she arrives."

Mitchel and Dobson shook hands, then the agent stood and left the helicopter. The door was closed. The engines whined as the helicopter lifted and started toward Kwanele's town.

It took several hours for Private Bates to drive the kids to Chester's house. It was dark out when the Hummer arrived. The front door opened.

"Are those your parents, Kwanele?" Chester asked.

Kwanele looked out the windshield and said, "What are they doing here?"

She took Kimmi's hand, opened the door, and hurried into her mother's arms. Chester was excited to see his family too but took his time getting out, careful to not show any excitement.

"Come in and get a drink or something," Chester said to Private Bates.

"I gotta get back to camp," he declined.

"Okay, but you have to meet my mom and Kwanele's parents first."

Bates turned off the engine, and they walked up to the house together. Rose grabbed her boy and hugged him until he squirmed loose.

"This is Private Bates," he introduced him to his mom. "He got me arrested."

Rose hugged him and thanked him for looking after her boys. Kwanele dragged him over to meet her parents and older brother. After a brief visit, Bates dismissed himself and drove back to base.

While the older people lingered outside talking, Kwanele brought Kimmi in to meet Chester's younger sister. They knelt on the floor in the living room and talked to Kimmi, and eventually the older people filed in.

Chester took Kwanele's brother to his room, and the adults sat down around the children.

It was established that the Sterling's would stay with the Thomas's for the weekend. They talked a bit about the aliens, how proud Mitchel was of everyone, and the discovery of Kimmi.

It grew late, and everyone started preparations for bed. Kwanele's bother stayed in Chester's room, her parents in the guest room, and Kwanele and Kimmi in Chester's sister's room.

When the lights had been turned off and everyone settled, they all heard the excited voice of Kwanele, "Mom! Come look what Kimmi can do!"

Thank you

Thank you for reading this book from Private Dragon publishing and games. We really appreciate your support. We want to know what you thought about this story, if you have a moment please let us know you felt by swiping to the next page at the end of this book if you are on digital or by leaving a review on Amazon or letting us know directly at https://privatedragon.com/

We have lots of books!

To learn more about other books that we are producing please visit our website at https://privatedragon.com/

About the Author

After several poetry writing assignments in a high school English class, Glen's teacher told him he was a wordsmith and to continue writing beyond school assignments. He found an opportunity to write for an audience when his sister asked for him to write some true stories for her to read to her son. That spawned a story about memories of their father's sock draw, which quickly took a fictitious turn to "The Sock Drawer Wands."